INDIANA JONES

and the

TEMPLE OF DOOM ™

The Storybook Based on the Film

Based on the film INDIANA JONES AND THE TEMPLE OF DOOM
Screenplay by Willard Huyck & Gloria Katz
Story by George Lucas
Storybook adaptation by Michael French

Published in the U.K. in Armada in 1984 by Fontana Paperbacks,
8 Grafton Street, London W1X 3LA.

TM and © 1984 Lucasfilm Ltd. (LFL). All rights reserved under
International and Pan-American Copyright Conventions. First
published in the U.S.A. in 1984 by Random House, Inc., New York,
and simultaneously in Canada by Random House of Canada Limited, Toronto.

ISBN 0 00 692405 0

Printed in Great Britain by
William Collins Sons & Co. Ltd., Glasgow

Willie Scott
A beautiful American
nightclub singer

Indiana Jones
A dedicated archeologist—
and a daring adventurer

Short Round
Indy's devoted young
Chinese sidekick

The Maharajah of Pankot
A powerful thirteen-year-old
Indian ruler

Mola Ram
The evil high priest
of the Thuggee cult

Chattar Lal
The scheming prime minister
of the Pankot Palace

Captain Blumburtt
A British cavalry
officer stationed
in India

Lao Che
A ruthless Chinese
crime lord

The Shaman of Mayapore
A visionary Indian
holy man

It was midnight in Shanghai. Even at this hour the great Chinese port on the Whangpoo River teemed with merchants, street peddlers, beggars, and thieves. Taxis and rickshaws carrying well-dressed couples to downtown nightclubs clattered over winding, narrow streets. On the surrounding hills, brightly tiled pagodas were silhouetted by the moon.

A hundred years ago Shanghai had been a sleepy market village. Now, in 1935, it was the centre of commerce for all of Asia. Businessmen and fortune hunters came here from around the world. They traded expensive silk, argued over the price of diamonds, and arranged to ship sugar and cotton to faraway ports.

That night an American in a dinner jacket appeared at the Club Obi Wan. The headwaiter sized him up as just another businessman and watched without interest as the American walked through the noisy, smoke-filled club to a corner table. Several impassive Chinese men sat waiting for him.

"Good evening, Dr. Jones," said the plump but muscular man at the head of the table. Lao Che was a notorious Shanghai crime lord, and his sons, sitting with him, were members of his gang. They all looked at the American coolly.

"Shall we finish our business?"

Indiana Jones asked, with equal reserve. For a moment he was distracted by the young woman singing on the nightclub stage. A pretty, frizzy-haired blonde, she wore a flowing red and gold lamé gown. An American, Indy realized. He wondered what she was doing so far from home.

"For this special occasion," Lao said, "I've ordered caviar and champagne. Something worthy of one of the world's great archeologists."

Indy watched as his Chinese host filled the round of glasses. He wasn't fooled by Lao's sudden friendliness, nor was he eager for small talk. He was tired from digging at nearby archeological sites. Very soon he would leave China and return to the university in the United States where he taught.

Indiana Jones really lived two lives. One was as a respected professor who fired the imagination of his students. The other was as an adventurer, tough and cool under pressure, who risked his life for rare archeological treasures. Usually he brought the pieces back to museums, but sometimes he sold them to individuals, if the price was fair.

"So, Dr. Jones, you've found Nurhachi for me?" Lao asked Indy.

"You know I did. Last night one of your boys tried to take Nurhachi without paying for him."

Lao dropped a bundle of notes on the table. When Indy frowned, he added several gold coins to the pile. "Now—I want Nurhachi."

As Indy peered at the gold coins he didn't notice Lao's eldest son sprinkle some powder into his champagne glass. "The diamond," Indy said, glancing up. He knew he could never trust Lao. "The deal was for the diamond."

Waiting out the silence, Indy was about to drink his champagne when the frizzy-haired singer strolled over to the table. "This is Miss Willie Scott," said Lao. Indy shook her hand. "And this is Indiana Jones," Lao added. "The famous archeologist."

Willie sat down and smiled flirtatiously. "An archeologist? Aren't you the guys who're always looking for your mummies?" she joked.

No one laughed. Everyone's attention was on Lao as he pulled the diamond out of his pocket and pushed it begrudgingly across the table. Indy examined the stone

carefully. Satisfied that it was real, he signalled to a nearby waiter, who brought over a small ornate jewellery box.

"Here he is," Indy said, and handed the box to Lao.

As he opened the box Lao's eyes widened at the pile of grey ashes. "At last! I have the remains of my ancestor, Nurhachi—the first emperor of the Manchu dynasty!"

Indy lifted his glass and drank his champagne. He was eager to clinch the deal and be done with Lao and his thugs. But after a moment his stomach began to burn bitterly, and Lao's smug face suddenly wavered before Indy's eyes. Indy put down the glass. "What did you do to me?" he asked shakily.

"You've been poisoned, Dr. Jones," said Lao, with a slow, triumphant smile. "And unless you hand back the diamond, I will not give you this antidote." He held up a small blue bottle of liquid.

For a moment Indy could only stare back helplessly.

"The poison works fast, Dr. Jones." Lao laughed, keeping the bottle in his hand. It was now or never, thought Indy. He lunged across the table for the antidote. Lao's youngest son pulled out a re-

volver. But Indy's weight tipped the table over, pushing the gunman against the wall.

The ashes of Nurhachi flew into the air, and the diamond and the gold coins spilled onto the floor and rolled toward the stage—along with the antidote. Indy scrambled after the bottle.

Gunshots rang out. Club patrons dived for cover. One bullet grazed Indy's shoulder and struck a huge brass gong on the stage. "Hey, what's going on?" cried Willie, more annoyed than frightened. The place was going bananas. Balloons were suddenly falling from the ceiling, people were screaming, and ice cubes were rolling across the floor from overturned champagne buckets.

Willie watched the handsome archeologist crawling on his hands and knees, groping for that funny little bottle. Nothing was making any sense. Then Willie spotted something on the floor that did.

"Gee, is that the diamond?" she whispered. She couldn't believe her luck. But as she reached down, two of Lao's thugs rushed toward the stone and knocked her away. All

Willie came up with was that little blue bottle.

"Stay there!" Indy shouted to Willie as bullets whistled past him. He managed to flip one of Lao's thugs onto a trolley and then took off after her. *Sorry, pal,* thought Willie, tucking the bottle into her dress and heading for the stage.

Sweat poured down Indy's face. His whole body was on fire. He dodged another bullet and crouched behind a potted palm. He had to find Willie, he realized, or he wouldn't have to worry about being killed by gunfire. The poison would do the job instead.

He made a dash for the stage, seized the sword from a statue of a Chinese warrior, and slashed the cords holding the mammoth brass gong. The gong fell to the stage with a deafening clang and Indy ducked behind it. Using it as a shield against the gunfire, he began to roll it toward a window. Just then Willie, heading for the exit, crossed his path. Indy pulled her behind the

gong and kept going as machine gun bullets sprayed across the room at them.

Willie yelped. Her dress was torn. She'd broken two nails. And now she was being kidnapped!

She screamed, but it was too late. The gong crashed through a huge stained glass window, and she and Indy flew out with it in a shower of broken glass. They plummeted down, bounced off an awning, and dropped into the back seat of a Duesenberg convertible.

"I don't believe this," Willie muttered. By some miracle she was still alive. The car roared off. She peered over the seat at the driver. A Chinese kid who didn't look more than ten years old was at the wheel.

"Step on it, Short Round," said Indy.

"Okey-doke, Indy," the kid said.

Indy reached into Willie's dress for the antidote and gulped it down.

"You don't look very good," Willie observed.

"Poison never agrees with me," Indy said dryly. Then, leaning forward, he called, "Pull a right, Shorty, and head for the bridge. That's the quickest way to the airport."

As the tyres squealed and Willie hung on for dear life, Indy looked out of the rear window. He was feeling better, but his problems were far from over. A large black car careered after them in pursuit.

"Faster, Shorty!" Indy ordered, then turned to Willie. "Short Round's my bodyguard."

"Bodyguard? He's just a kid!"

Short Round frowned, making sure Willie saw him through the rearview mirror.

"We met in Shanghai," Indy explained. "When he was trying to pick my pocket. I'm taking him to the States."

"This is all very interesting," Willie said, "but I think I've had enough. First you kidnap me. Then you throw me through a window. And now you've got half of Shanghai chasing us. Just look at me." She straightened her dress and patted down her hair. "Where are we going, anyway?"

"Siam," said Indy.

"Siam? I'm not dressed for Siam!" Three bullets whizzed past her ear and hit the dashboard. Willie dropped to the floor.

When they reached the airport, they quickly jumped out of the car and boarded a waiting cargo plane. It was off the ground before the pursuing gunmen could stop them. When they arrived in Siam, Indy knew, they could catch a connecting flight to the States. Indy had anticipated trouble from Lao, but not the addition of Miss Scott to his journey. In Siam he'd give her some money and she'd be on her own.

The accommodations in the cargo plane were hardly first-class. There were no seats, and coops with live chickens were scattered everywhere. It was freezing cold, too. Indy gave Willie a blanket, then changed into his khaki pants and leather jacket. Using his trusted bullwhip as a pillow, he lay down to sleep, peacefully unaware that the plane he'd chartered was owned

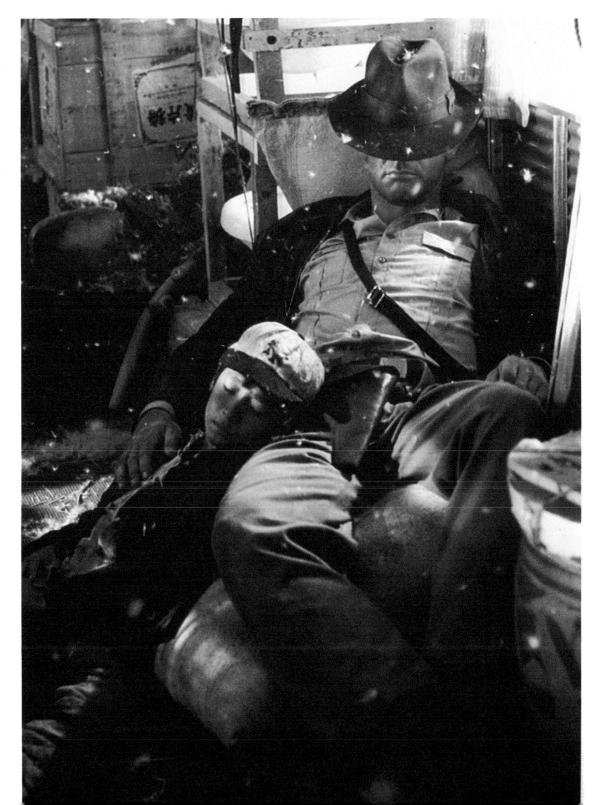

by Lao Che's freight company. Only minutes earlier, when his sons had failed to stop Indy at the airport, Lao had radioed the pilot. The crime lord's message was angry and to the point: Get rid of Dr. Jones and his friends!

When their passengers were fast asleep, the pilot and co-pilot sneaked back to the cargo hold. The blond girl, the young boy, and the gentleman with the rugged face looked peaceful and innocent. The pilots began to argue. Neither had the courage to carry out Lao's orders. But they feared Lao Che. They knew their own lives were in danger if they disappointed him. There was more arguing before they thought of a solution. Quickly they emptied the fuel from the tanks, strapped on parachutes, and tiptoed past their sleeping passengers to the plane door.

Cold air hit Willie like a slap in the face, waking her. She opened her eyes to see the two pilots leaping from the plane. "I wonder who's flying this thing," she mused. Then she screamed in panic.

"There's nobody flying the plane!" she yelled, shaking Indy awake.

He rose groggily and watched the parachutes streaming through the air below them in the dawn light. "Calm down," he told Willie. He made his way to the cockpit, slipped into the pilot's seat, and checked the instrument panel. Everything looked okay. Suddenly his eyes darted to the fuel gauge. "Uh-oh."

"What is it?" said Willie.

"We've got a problem."

"What kind of problem?"

"We're out of fuel." Indy hurried back to the cargo hold and bumped into Short Round.

"I already check, Indy," he said. "No more parachute."

Short Round watched, puzzled, as Indy searched the overhead compartments again. As the propellers froze and the plane dipped in the sky, Willie began to scream from the cockpit. Short Round was afraid too, but he refused to worry. He trusted Indy. Since their meeting in Shanghai, they'd been through a lot of adventures together, and Indy always saved the day.

Indy was not only a hero to Short Round, he was almost like a father to him. Short Round's parents had been killed long ago in a war with the Japanese, and the boy had been put in one orphanage after another before he took to living in the streets. That's when he'd tried to pick Indy's pockets.

"Quick—give me a hand," Indy called to Short Round as he wrestled with a deflated life raft in one of the compartments.

Willie was suddenly beside them. "Are you crazy?" she screeched. "A life raft? We're not sinking—we're crashing!"

Indy didn't have time to argue. The plane had gone into a nose dive. Below, jagged, snow-capped peaks loomed up. Indy shouted instructions as they all hurried to the open plane door. Short Round and Willie held the raft, and Indy grasped the cord that would inflate it. The plane dropped lower and lower, until the snow on the mountains looked close enough to touch.

"Now!" shouted Indy.

The three jumped out of the plane, hanging on to the raft. In midair Indy pulled the cord. The raft puffed up like a blowfish and hurtled into the snow. Then it rocketed down the mountain, skidding first over snow, then through thickets of trees and over rocks. Gaining speed, it plunged off a cliff and into a river, rushed downstream, and finally drifted into a calm pond. There it came to a stop.

Willie thought she was dead. Then her eyes opened and she was staring into the face of a skinny, dark man in a tattered robe.

She yelped and drew back, then turned to Indy. "Where are we, anyway?"

"India," he answered as he helped Short Round out of the raft. "And this gentleman is probably a shaman."

"What's a shaman?" asked Willie, keeping her distance.

"Sort of a village medicine man," Indy replied. "Half high priest, half doctor."

Indy spoke to the shaman in a Hindi dialect. The conversation continued for several minutes as the shaman kept pointing to the sky. Willie was surprised that Indy could communicate with the man at all. "What did he say?" she finally asked.

"He said his people were expecting me. They were waiting at the river for the plane to fall down." Indy was as puzzled as Willie by the shaman's response, but there was no use in speculating.

"Did he tell you exactly where we are?" asked Willie.

Indy nodded. "We're in an area

called the Mayapore hills. It's not too far from New Delhi. We'll rest up in his village, then leave for Delhi tomorrow."

Short Round was relieved that they weren't hopelessly lost. But as he entered the shaman's village he grew uneasy. The villagers looked half starved. Their thatched-roof houses were falling down. And when Short Round passed a group of women, they reached out to touch him, crying. Then he realized something very odd. The village had no children. Perplexed, Short Round asked Indy what was wrong.

"You got me, Shorty," he answered, troubled himself as he glanced around. It was as though some disaster had hit the village.

Indy walked over to the shaman.

"What's happened here?" he asked. "A drought? A famine?"

The shaman's face was pained as he spoke. "An evil has fallen on our village. The evil starts in Pankot. Then, like monsoon, it moves darkness over our land."

"Evil? What evil?" asked Indy, confused. "And what's Pankot?"

"Pankot Palace," the shaman replied.

"Oh," said Indy, starting to remember his history.

Until 1830, the Pankot Palace had been the home of an Indian maharajah and his family. Then the British had driven the maharajah off, leaving the palace deserted. "How can an empty palace be evil?" Indy asked the shaman.

"Palace no longer empty. New

maharajah lives there. He brings the evil. You must stop it."

"Me? I think you have the wrong guy," Indy said, starting to turn away.

"Our god, Krishna, promise that man would drop out of sky to help us." The shaman smiled suddenly at Indy. "You."

Great, thought Indy as he translated the shaman's message for Willie and Short Round.

"You mean there's really a palace around here?" Willie exclaimed. For a moment she felt some hope. Maybe she could find fresh clothes there, and some decent food. Then she asked uneasily, "But what's this about an evil maharajah? What did he do?"

Indy spoke with the shaman for another minute before he answered Willie. "The maharajah's men stole the *sivalinga* from this village," he explained. "That's a sacred stone. I've seen one or two in

museums. The villagers believe that the sacred stone protects them from evil. Once the stone was taken, their wells went dry. Crops turned bad. Animals died. People got sick . . ."

"Nice guy, that maharajah," Short Round said. "Why he take the stone, Indy?"

"He wanted the villagers to pray to his god. An evil god, the shaman says. When the villagers refused, he grabbed the stone."

"I'll bet that stone business is just superstition," said Willie. She paused, thinking. "It wasn't a diamond, was it?"

"Maybe it's superstition," Indy said reflectively, "maybe not. But *something* terrible happened to this village." As Indy glanced around he felt bad for the people. But what could he do to help? Krishna or not, he was already late for the new term at the university. "There's one thing that really bothers me," Indy

said, looking at Short Round. "Notice there are no kids around here?"

Short Round nodded. "Everyone stare at me, like I'm special . . ." No one had ever looked at him that way.

"There's good reason," said Indy. "According to the shaman, one night not long ago a fire started mysteriously in the fields. The men in the village went to put it out. When they returned, the women were crying. All their children had been kidnapped by the maharajah's men."

"But why?" asked Short Round, feeling uneasy.

"No one knows," Indy said.

"But that's not *our* problem," Willie protested. "I mean, who's in charge of this country, anyway?"

"The British," Indy told her. "They're the only ones who can really help. But the shaman and the village chief have already spoken to some British officers. So far nothing's been done."

"Meaning?" said Willie.

"Meaning that the villagers expect us to help them. Krishna promised them we would find the stone and bring back their children."

Willie shook her head in disbelief. "You didn't say we would, did you?"

"I only promised that when we got to Delhi, I'd speak to some friends and they would investigate."

Willie couldn't wait to leave in the morning. What a mess she was in. Hungry, dirty, and in the company of a loony archeologist. Her parents would have a fit if they knew. They thought she was crazy when she ran off to sing in a Chinese nightclub. But with the Depression there wasn't much work in the

States, and she'd always craved a little adventure. That was, until she met Indiana Jones!

Indy turned in early that night, but he slept poorly. He thought he was having a nightmare when he heard crashing sounds outside and something rushing into the village. Then, as he hurried out of his hut, a young boy, starved and emaciated, collapsed in his arms.

The boy whispered into Indy's ear, his voice so weak that only one word was clear: "Sankara." Slowly his bleeding fist opened to drop something into Indy's hand. It was a tattered piece of cloth that looked like a fragment from a painting or a manuscript page.

The villagers rushed from their huts, weeping joyfully that one of their children had returned. But Indy didn't feel any joy as he studied the boy. His wrists and ankles were badly cut, as if he'd been chained. Whip marks covered his back. His ribs poked through his paper-thin skin. Who had done this? Indy grew angrier by the second. He knew one thing: Delhi would have to wait a few days. Tomorrow he would set out for the Pankot Palace.

With the first rays of dawn the villagers loaded three elephants with supplies, and a guide promised to lead Indy to the maharajah's palace. Willie was annoyed at the change of plans, but hardly surprised. Another crazy adventure, she thought as she unsteadily tried to mount her elephant. She couldn't believe she'd actually have to ride this thing! But the idea of meeting a genuine maharajah improved her spirits. Maharajahs were supposed to have lots of money, not to mention jewellery.

Late the next day, as Indy, Willie, and Short Round pushed through the dense jungle, Indy pulled out the piece of cloth that the boy had given him the night before in the village. It was covered with faint writing and depicted an old man. *Probably the priest Sankara,* thought Indy. That was the name the boy had whispered.

He peered closely at the cloth. The characters were dim, but he recognized the legend of Sankara written there. According to Hindu legend, the god Shiva had given Sankara five magical stones to help the priest combat evil. But that was centuries ago, and no one knew what had happened to the mysterious stones since that time. *Lost?*

Stolen? Indy thought to himself.

At that moment, just as he and the others approached a clearing, their guide abruptly stopped his elephant. Indy saw that his face was rigid with fear. As everyone came to a halt Indy dismounted slowly, followed by Willie and Short Round. In the clearing, smiling evilly, was a small stone statue of a hideous woman with a twisted face and four snakelike arms. It was Kali, the Hindu goddess of death and destruction, Indy knew.

"Everybody stay back!" he shouted as he moved closer to the statue. It was so grotesque, so terrifying, that there was little point in making Willie and Short Round face it. Indy could only wonder what a

totem of Kali was doing in the middle of nowhere. When he turned to ask the guide, the frightened man was jabbering in Hindi and driving all the elephants away.

With a grim smile, Indy faced his companions. "From here on we walk," he said.

Short Round and Willie didn't respond. There in the distance, rising above the jungle, was a magnificent alabaster palace. Spellbound,

Indy studied the Pankot Palace. It was hard for him to believe that a monument so splendid could harbour evil. It was too regal, too beautiful.

When they'd struggled up the mountain and reached the palace entrance, they found two lines of Indian guards in elegant uniforms, their curved swords tucked into red sashes. The guards watched silently as the three visitors entered an empty courtyard of ornately carved marble. "Hello?" Indy called, only to hear his echo.

Then a crisp voice answered, "I would say you look rather lost."

A severe-looking Indian in an English suit appeared from nowhere. He glanced disdainfully at the mud-splattered intruders as if they hardly belonged in a palace.

"Lost?" Indy smiled broadly. "Hardly. We're on our way to Delhi and need accommodations for the night. This is Miss Scott . . . and Mr. Round. I'm Indiana Jones."

"Dr. Jones? The eminent archeologist?" The man warmed immediately. "I'm Chattar Lal. Prime Minister for His Highness, the Maharajah of Pankot. May I welcome you to the palace . . ."

"You mean we can stay here?" Willie exclaimed. Chattar Lal nodded graciously, then invited them to dine with the maharajah. It was to be a banquet for other guests as well. Willie couldn't wait. She was hungry enough to eat a horse, though she'd prefer a steak and a baked potato.

That evening the three joined Chattar Lal in the garden before dinner. Indy looked the maharajah's guests over. There were Indian merchants, court ministers, and a British cavalry captain in uniform. Indy introduced himself to Captain Blumburtt.

"I saw your troops come in at sunset," Indy said casually.

"Just a routine inspection," Blumburtt said. "We have to keep an eye on our empire, you know."

Suddenly Indy's attention turned

to a table covered with religious devotional objects. He picked one up carefully. "Haven't seen one of these in years," he said.

"What is it?" Blumburtt asked.

"It's called a krtya. Like the voodoo dolls of West Africa. The krtya represents your enemy—and gives you complete power over him."

"A lot of mumbo jumbo," the captain huffed.

"Not for someone who believes in it," Indy said.

When dinner was announced, the guests marched into a long hall with a low table and pillows for seats.

Short Round flopped down, chewing his gum. So far he was unimpressed with the riches of the palace. And everybody acted like a big shot, like they thought the palace was the greatest thing since fried rice. Well, what was so great about sitting on pillows? Hadn't they heard of chairs?

Two ornate silver doors swung open. Chattar Lal rose from the table. "May I introduce His Supreme Highness, the Maharajah of Pankot . . ."

Short Round looked twice. The figure strolling through the doors

was only slightly taller than he, and at most only a year or two older. Willie and Indy were startled too. The young maharajah bowed solemnly to his guests.

Indy bowed in return, as did the other guests. Only Short Round refused to bow or take off his hat. When Indy gave him a stern look across the table, Short Round finally lowered his head, but he didn't like it. Just because this kid was dressed in a fancy robe covered with jewels and ruled a palace and had dozens of servants . . . Short Round knew he could outwrestle and outrun the maharajah any day of the week.

"May I ask a question?" Indy said to the prime minister as everyone waited to be served. "While I was looking over the maharajah's artifacts, I noticed a small wooden monkey next to the krtya. It was carved quite recently, I think. Wasn't the monkey an image worshipped by the Thuggee cult?"

"Once upon a time, yes," Chattar Lal answered. His tone was polite but cold. "But that's ancient history. The monkey is quite old, just like the krtya. Today they're nothing but harmless charms."

"Then what about the statue of Kali I saw in the clearing near the palace?" Indy ventured. "Is that a harmless charm too?"

"Exactly," the prime minister said, forcing a smile.

"I wouldn't worry, old man," Blumburtt said to Indy. "The Thuggees have been gone for a century. Granted, they were a menace in their time. Greatly feared. They stole, they terrorized the locals. And they held bizarre religious rituals. A rather violent, fanatical lot, I'm afraid. Said to have special powers—evil powers. But we did drive them off, you know, along with Kali and their other nasty gods."

As the first course was served, Willie closed her eyes in anticipation. The food, whatever it was,

smelled divine. She smiled as she looked down. On her plate the boiled boa constrictor seemed to be smiling back. Willie stifled a scream. It was bad enough that the maharajah had turned out to be a kid, dashing her dreams, but couldn't he even serve decent food?

The second course was a plate of large fried beetles, whose legs stuck out like toothpicks. The Indian merchant next to Willie crunched on one greedily. "But you're not eating," he said.

"I, uh, had bugs for lunch," said Willie. She stood up and managed three steps before fainting dead away.

After helping Willie back to her room, Indy and Short Round finished their dinner and thanked the maharajah for his hospitality. As they left the banquet hall Indy spotted Chattar Lal in the hallway. The prime minister was whispering urgently to a robed figure whose hood partially concealed his face. A moment later the mysterious stranger turned and vanished. Something was going on, thought Indy. Tonight's dinner made him suspicious too. Roasted boar had been served for the main course, yet no devout Hindu ever touched meat.

Before retiring for the night Indy ducked into the palace kitchen, grabbed some fruit, and made his way to Willie's room. She sat up on her bed and eyed the fresh oranges and bananas gratefully. "At last," she breathed, taking the fruit from Indy. "Real food!"

"Are you okay?" Indy asked.

"So far. But I think I'd like to leave this place—soon. It's creepy."

"Sleep tight," Indy said. "I'll see you in the morning."

When he returned to his room, Indy found Short Round snoring softly on the other bed. He smiled at the boy and pulled the sheet up to cover him. Then his glance jumped to his own bed. A mural of sinister men dressed in robes and turbans hung above the headboard. It was enough to give anyone nightmares, Indy thought.

As Indy paced restlessly around the room, a robed figure behind him appeared to come to life. Indy pivoted quickly, but the assassin already had a cord around Indy's neck.

"Shorty!" Indy gasped.

The boy slept soundly. Indy tried to slip the assassin off his back, but the man hung on, pulling the cord even tighter. Indy fell to the floor. He could hardly breathe. His hand groped for a heavy copper pot. With the last of his strength he swung the pot at the assassin's head. The blow stunned the man and he tumbled back, releasing the cord.

Short Round woke up and tossed Indy his bullwhip. Recovering, the assassin pulled a knife from his sash. His face suddenly went blank and his eyes widened to a hateful glare. Indy had never seen anything like it. Uneasy, he coiled his whip and sent it flying.

The whip wrapped around the assassin's neck like a noose. His face began to redden. But with his tremendous strength he jerked the whip handle from Indy's hands. It flew into the air.

For a moment the assassin grinned victoriously. Then his face dissolved into confusion. The whip handle had caught in the overhead fan. As the fan took hold it lifted the giant off the floor, twirling him around, faster and faster, until he was dead.

"Shorty, turn off the fan," Indy said. "I'm going to check on Willie."

He hurried down the hall and

burst into her room. Willie woke with a start. "What is it?" she cried fearfully.

But Indy didn't respond. He was too busy looking the room over, opening closet doors and rapping on walls. Suddenly he felt a draft and pushed on a carved pillar. The wall behind it creaked loudly and slid inward, revealing the entrance to a tunnel.

Frightened, Willie pulled her covers up to her chin. Cold air whistled into the room. Indy peered inside. He could make out an inscription at the front of the tunnel. In Sanskrit it told the story of the priest Sankara and how the god Shiva had given him five magical stones. Indy pulled out the piece of cloth that the boy had given him in the village. It was the same inscription, word for word.

"Shorty, get our gear," Indy said as the boy appeared in the doorway. "We're going exploring. Willie, you stay here."

Indy stuffed his whip in his shoulder pouch and led Short Round behind the fake wall and into total blackness. He felt his way along a narrow tunnel. The passage was cold and draughty and seemed to go deeper and deeper into the earth.

Short Round suddenly felt something hard and crunchy on the tunnel floor. "I step on something!" he whispered.

Indy struck a match and pulled back in horror. The floor was carpeted with live insects, tens of thousands of them. Indy and Short Round kicked at them in panic, but they kept crawling back. "And I thought snakes were bad," Indy muttered.

Indy spotted an oily rag on the floor and lit it. A large room sat just

off the tunnel, free of insects. Indy and Short Round scurried inside. As they were catching their breath, the door slammed closed behind them.

"Oh, no," Indy said, going to the door. He pounded on it futilely. Then he raised his voice. "Willie! Get down here!"

Short Round listened for an answer, but all he heard was a rumbling sound. The floor began to vibrate. He watched, terrified, as sharp spikes rose up under their feet. Then, after more rumbling from above, a set of gleaming spikes shot out of the ceiling and inched toward them.

Short Round huddled with Indy in a corner. The ceiling spikes glistened as they edged closer. Indy looked frantically for a lever to open the door. Nothing. Suddenly they heard Willie's voice.

"Indy, where are you? I'm coming . . . but I can't see much . . . there's stuff all over the floor . . . ahhh! Bugs!"

Willie's screams rang through the tunnel.

"Willie—shut up and listen!" Indy ordered. "There's a door . . . and somewhere there should be a lever." The ceiling spikes moved closer, almost touching their heads. "Come on, Willie . . . you can do it . . . "

"I can't," she whispered.

"You have to!"

Short Round closed his eyes. He was going to die, he thought, but somehow he wasn't afraid. He was with Indy, and that comforted him. An old Chinese prayer was coming to mind when the terrible creaking stopped. The door popped open and Willie ducked inside, brushing bugs out of her hair and clothes.

As she looked at the spikes in amazement her elbow accidentally touched a protruding rock. At this the ceiling spikes began to descend again. At the same instant another door in the tunnel rolled open and a wind howled toward them like a note of gloomy music. The three dashed out of the spike chamber and clustered around the windy opening.

"Here goes nothing," Indy said after a moment as he ducked into the inky passage. Willie and Short Round stumbled after him. The tunnel widened and continued into the mountain, and they heard soft chanting ahead. Soon a reddish light guided them to the mouth of the tunnel. Indy crawled to the lip and gazed down. Short Round and Willie peeked over his shoulder.

A sprawling subterranean temple carved out of solid rock lay below. Hundreds of chanting Indians bowed and swayed before a huge statue of Kali, whose face, frozen in rage, loomed above them. A massive stone altar sat by her feet, and in front of it burned a wide pit of molten lava, its flames spitting up angrily.

As the three of them stared down, more worshippers streamed in, heads bowed, and priests in long, dark robes appeared on balconies overlooking the altar. On each side of the altar were dark, narrow chambers with vaulted ceilings, guarded by statues of demigods, half man and half beast. As Indy listened the chanting grew louder. An eerie wind howled above it, a music unto itself.

"What's going on?" Willie asked.

"It's a temple of death," Indy whispered. "And this is a Thuggee ceremony. They're worshipping Kali."

Short Round watched, wide-eyed, as rows of robed priests moved from the dark chambers toward the altar. They dragged with them a man, struggling like a wild animal, and tied him to an iron frame hanging above the altar.

"One of the Thuggee rituals is human sacrifice," Indy said grimly. "The victim's blood has a special use afterward. When an innocent person drinks it, he falls under Kali's influence."

Indy warned Short Round to turn his eyes from the sacrifice. Willie looked on, sickened. Slowly, a tall priest approached the altar. He was the same man that Indy had seen talking to Chattar Lal in the hallway after dinner. The pale, sinister face and sunken eyes were the picture of evil. The priest held up three brightly coloured stones to the worshippers, then solemnly placed them on the altar.

"Mola Ram!" the crowd shouted to the priest. "Mola Ram!"

As he heard his name the high priest raised his arms to the congregation. The smoke from the lava

pit drifted toward the stones. Brought together, they ignited like white, glowing embers.

Indy watched, fascinated. Everything was starting to make sense. "Remember the missing stone from the Mayapore village?" he whispered to Short Round and Willie. "The villagers knew their rock was magic, but they didn't know it was one of the lost Sankara Stones."

"What are they?" Short Round asked.

Indy related the Hindu legend, but Short Round was still puzzled. "Indy, why stones shine so bright?" he asked.

"The legend says that when the Sankara Stones are brought to-

gether, the diamonds inside of them will glow."

Willie's eyes widened. "Diamonds?" She gazed down raptly at the altar.

"I'm not leaving the palace until I have those stones," Indy whispered. "One for the villagers, and the others for a museum."

The three waited uneasily as the priests and worshippers began to disperse. When the last priest had left, leaving the temple empty, Indy turned to his friends. "All right, now, listen. You two stay here and keep quiet."

Short Round didn't argue. He was in no hurry to get any closer to that monstrous statue. He watched as

Indy clambered down a carved stone column and cautiously approached the bright pit of molten lava. The flames lit the gruesome face of Kali, making her seem almost alive. On the altar the stones still gave off a white glow.

Studying the lava pit, Indy realized it was too wide to jump across. He uncoiled his whip and flung it over the chasm, letting the end wrap around the tusk of a stone elephant. He tested the whip for strength, then swung himself across and landed safely. As he neared the altar his face glowed in the reflection of the stones. Boldly, he picked one up. Instead of burning him, the stone sparkled softly in his hand. Dazzled, he peered into it for a moment and then dropped all three into his shoulder pouch. He turned, about to head back to Willie and

Short Round, when an echo rose from the other side of the altar. He listened, startled, and then moved toward the noise.

Short Round held his breath as Indy disappeared behind the altar. Whatever Indy was doing, Short Round wished he'd hurry back. Every second they spent in the temple was a second too long. He turned to check on Willie when suddenly he heard distant footsteps. Then he saw the lengthening shadows on the tunnel wall. He grabbed for a dagger he kept under his belt as two Thuggee guards rushed toward him.

"Run, Willie, run!" Short Round yelled, pushing her out of the way. One guard lunged at Short Round, and the other grabbed Willie. She kneed him in the stomach and kept running. Short Round jabbed his

dagger at his attacker, missed, and tried to flee. The other Thuggee seized him roughly by the neck, letting him dangle in the air, and laughed. Fear hit Short Round like a cold, hard rock. His only hope was that Willie would get help.

As Indy skirted around the altar, he was drawn to a grey shaft of light rising through a hole in the dirt floor. He peered down through the dust, mystified, and found himself staring into a mine. Dimly lit paths crisscrossed one another and led away to large tunnels. There, dozens of emaciated children dressed in rags, their legs chained together, were digging with picks and shovels. Other children, also chained, were dragging sacks of dirt to railroad mine cars. Fat, evil-looking Thuggee guards yelled at them to move faster.

The missing Mayapore children!

Indy thought. They had become slaves for the Thuggees.

But what could they be digging for? A little girl with a grimy face, too weak to lift a sack of dirt, suddenly collapsed on the railroad tracks. No sooner had she fallen than a bare-chested guard walked up and kicked her. Indy flinched. He couldn't control himself. He reached for a rock and hurled it at the guard. Startled, a dozen small heads twisted up to stare at Indy.

Then, as Indy moved closer to the hole, the earth around him sagged under his weight. He tumbled helplessly into the mine and, looking up, saw that he was surrounded by temple guards. They dragged him roughly into a small holding cell, where Short Round and several other boys were in chains.

"Getting caught not my fault, Indy," said Short Round. "But Willie ran fast. Maybe she get help."

"Don't worry," Indy said. "We'll get out of here somehow." He glanced over to one of the boys in the cell. "What's your name?" asked Indy.

The tall, gangly boy looked back fearfully. "Nainsukh," he finally answered, as if deciding he could trust Indy.

"What are you doing here?"

"I too old to work in mine, too tall for low tunnels. Now the evil of Kali will take me."

"What do you mean?"

"They will make me drink blood of Kali—then I fall into black sleep of Kali Ma. I become like them. I live in a nightmare. Never wake up . . ."

The boy suddenly turned quiet, moving in fear to the back of the cell as the door clanged open. Two burly guards moved toward Indy and Short Round and then herded them down a dark, winding passage. They were led into the chamber of the high priest, Mola Ram.

The priest's walls were covered with Thuggee devotional objects, and in front of Indy, on a small altar, was another statue of Kali. The three Sankara Stones had been taken from Indy's shoulder pouch and placed before Kali on the altar. Eyes closed in meditation, Mola Ram sat cross-legged before the goddess.

Suddenly the priest opened his eyes and glared at the intruders. "Dr. Jones," he said, "you were caught trying to steal the Sankara Stones."

Indy had difficulty meeting the priest's repulsive stare. "Nobody's perfect," he said, looking at the stones on the altar. They were glowing softly.

Mola Ram, noticing Indy's fascination, spoke again. "There were five stones in the beginning, Dr. Jones. Over the centuries they were lost in wars, sold by thieves, or hoarded by the superstitious—like the villagers you visited. Now we have three of the stones back. The other two are buried somewhere beneath the temple. When the British raided the Pankot Palace, a priest loyal to Kali hid the stones there . . ."

"Is that what the children are digging for?" asked Indy angrily.

"That, and for gems that we

sell to support our cause."

"They're slaves!"

"They're servants of Kali," Mola Ram corrected him, and nodded to the guards. "Your young friend will join our workers in the mines. As for you, Dr. Jones, you will become a true believer."

Indy blinked as he remembered the human sacrifice in the temple. He was afraid but determined not to show it. "True believer?" he said nonchalantly. "What's that supposed to mean?"

"You will drink the blood of one of Kali's victims. You will become one of us."

The guards grabbed Indy and tied

him to the statue just as the maharajah entered the chamber, smiling arrogantly. Indy shook his head. "So you're one of them too," he said.

"You will not suffer, Dr. Jones. I recently became of age and tasted the blood of Kali."

"That's nice to know," said Indy. "But, personally, I'm not drinking a single drop."

From his pocket the maharajah pulled a krtya, crudely shaped to resemble Indy, and without warning dipped it into a flaming urn. Indy cried out in pain.

The maharajah smiled again. "Dr. Jones, have you changed your mind?"

"Fat chance for that," Indy said defiantly. Incensed, the maharajah glared at him. Then, strangely, his face went blank, as if he were in a trance. He nodded to a guard, who stripped off Indy's jacket as the maharajah picked up Indy's bull-whip. He lashed out, and Indy arched in pain.

Short Round winced as he watched the second blow. How could they do this to Indy? Short Round's anger overwhelmed him. With the third blow, he broke away from his guard. But before Short Round could attack, the maharajah pivoted and lashed the whip at him, cutting him on the cheek and stunning him. "You deserve that and more," the maharajah said to Short Round. Then he turned to the guards. "Take him to the mines!"

As Short Round was carried away Mola Ram approached Indy. He was carrying a human skull full of blood. Indy fought as a guard forced his mouth open.

"Do not resist, Dr. Jones," Mola Ram warned. "It will do you no good. Kali will soon rule your soul. She will rule all of India. It is inevitable. Then the Hindus will bow to her, as will the Hebrews, the Christians . . . "

The whip in the maharajah's hand lashed out again and Indy grimaced in pain. But he wasn't about to submit, not in a million years.

Willie rushed, out of breath, through the secret door and into her room. She had to find help quickly. There was no telling what the guards had done with Short Round, and maybe Indy was in trouble too. Frantically she brushed insects off her arm and stumbled into the hallway. Nobody was around. She searched the courtyard next, but it, too, was deserted. Growing more anxious, she returned to her room and drew back with a start. Chattar Lal was standing by the tunnel entrance, staring at her oddly. His face was cold and detached.

"Oh, Prime Minister," Willie gasped. "An hour ago ... Short Round and Indy found a secret passage. It led to a temple of death ... people worshipping Kali. And some poor man was being sacrificed—"

"Yes," Chattar Lal interrupted, moving closer to Willie. "He was."

Willie tried to resist as the prime minister seized her by the arm, but he was overpowering. She stared back in disbelief. Chattar Lal was a Thuggee too! Probably everyone in the palace belonged to the cult! She struggled in vain as two guards shoved her inside the tunnel and led her into the temple. It was filled with worshippers, and the loud, strange chanting rang in her ears. She went rigid with fear as her wrists and ankles were manacled and she was thrown into a crude iron cage in front of the lava pit.

She was going to be sacrificed, she realized, trembling. She was going to die. Suddenly she spotted Indy by the priest's chamber, next to Mola Ram. At the same instant she managed to slip her slender wrist out of one of the manacles.

"Indy!" she shouted. "Help me! Indy—"

Mola Ram and the other priests looked on without emotion as Indy approached Willie. The fierce heat from the lava pit, and the fear welling up inside her, made Willie dizzy. Still, she managed to stretch out her hand to Indy. He would save her now, and take her from this terrible nightmare. Indy stood before her for a moment, smiling in understanding, and then, as his smile abruptly died, he took her wrist and snapped the manacle back around it.

Down in the bowels of the mountain Short Round struggled with a pick as a Thuggee guard stood nearby keeping close watch. His feet were chained together so that he could hardly move, and he felt exhausted. His muscles weren't used to strenuous labour, and the air was too dirty to breathe. The guard had struck him twice with his rifle for moving too slowly.

Wearily Short Round sliced his pick into the tunnel wall. When he jerked it away, a stream of molten lava gushed toward him, hissing like a snake. Short Round jumped clear, but the Thuggee guard was too slow. Hot lava swept over his foot, and his face contorted in pain.

After a minute, when his pain eased, the guard looked around the mine, bewildered, as if he had no idea where he was. The cold fury in his face, his blank, empty stare, had vanished. He seemed, suddenly, like a completely different person. *The fire!* thought Short Round. Had the pain of the fiery lava really woken the guard from the nightmare of Kali? He decided to find out. After the injured guard was dragged away by two others, Short Round picked up a heavy rock and hit his leg manacles repeatedly with it. The rusted chains finally broke under the blows.

Quickly he slipped away and

crouched behind a mine car. Above him he could hear the temple filling with worshippers. He listened again. Willie's screams echoed down into the mines.

The boy felt his stomach tighten. Willie was obviously in trouble, and he could only guess about Indy.

Short Round raced through several tunnels, hiding whenever he heard the leaden footsteps of Thuggees. After he'd found Indy's whip and shoulder pouch, Short Round hurried back to the hole in the tunnel roof that led up to the temple. The other children watched him in silent amazement, as if what they were seeing were an illusion. No one ever escaped from the mines. Ignoring their stares, Short Round found a ladder and scurried up to the temple.

Moving swiftly, he crawled behind the altar and peeked out. Hundreds of worshippers chanted and swayed in a frenzy. The three Sankara Stones blazed at the feet of Kali. Short Round watched, horrified, as Willie stood on the edge of the fiery pit. He went cold. They were going to sacrifice her! He started to rush out but caught himself. Only Indy had a chance of rescuing Willie—if he was around.

Short Round's gaze jumped to the line of priests emerging from the chamber. As they filed in he saw that Indy was in their midst, his handsome face now blank and impassive. Short Round groaned. How had it happened? Mola Ram must have made Indy drink the blood. Indy was a Thuggee now!

There was only one thing to do. He had to wake Indy from the trance of Kali, just as he'd seen the guard awakened. And he had to move quickly, before anything happened to Willie.

Rows of torches flared brightly along the temple walls. Ducking as he ran, Short Round reached the first torch and seized it. Then he charged through the guards and priests and thrust the flame toward Indy.

Indy saw him coming. With one hand he knocked Short Round away, as easily as if he were brushing off a fly, and the boy skidded helplessly across the temple floor. Stunned, Short Round felt like crying. Indy was glaring at him with cold hatred, as if the two had never met, as if Indy wanted to choke the breath out of him. For a moment Short Round stared back, paralyzed with disbelief and hurt. But he knew he couldn't give up. He raised himself and charged again.

With all his strength he drove the flaming torch into Indy's leg. Indy dropped to the floor, writhing in pain. At the same moment an angry guard seized Short Round by the neck and brought a knife to the boy's throat.

"Hold it," Indy said to the guard, picking himself up. "He's mine."

The temple fell silent as Indy marched toward his victim. Mola Ram and Chattar Lal looked on in anticipation. This would be a true test of Dr. Jones's allegiance to Kali.

Indy's powerful hands gripped Short Round's small shoulders. Then, just for an instant, he winked. "I'm all right, Shorty," he whispered. "You ready?" Short Round winked back.

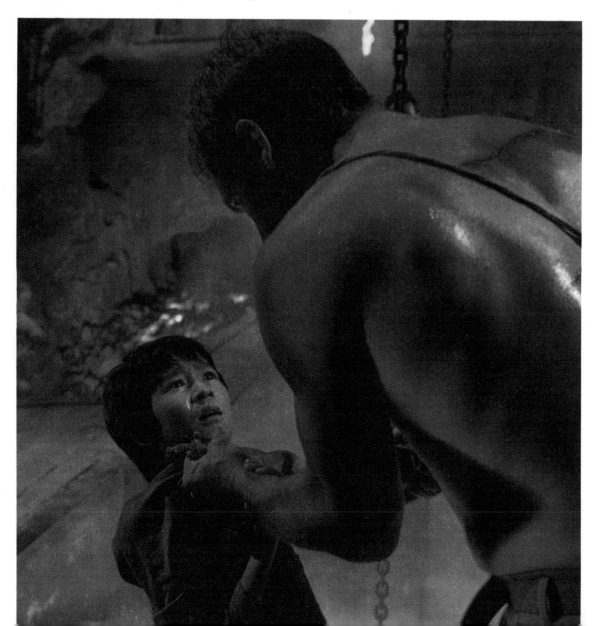

Suddenly Indy twisted around and swung a fist into the nearest priest, who reeled back and knocked down a second. Short Round whirled fearlessly and gave a karate kick to an approaching guard, then grabbed a torch to hold off several more. Indy raced over to help Willie. Chained to a large metal wheel that was about to descend into the lava pit, she was so paralyzed with fear that she barely recognized Indy as he helped her squeeze out of her manacles.

As he led Willie from the pit, Indy heard rushing footsteps behind him. He turned just in time to see Chattar Lal's angry face and the knife in his raised hand. Deftly Indy blocked the knife, turned sideways, and watched as Chattar Lal lost his balance and plunged, screaming, into the pit.

Then Indy dashed to the altar, grabbed the Sankara Stones, and dropped them into his shoulder pouch. When he turned back to the temple, the worshippers were fleeing in panic.

"What we do now, Indy?" asked Short Round.

Indy's face hardened with determination. "We're going to get those kids out of here," he said.

As soon as Willie revived, Indy led her and Short Round back into the mine.

They skirted past a string of loaded mine cars and hid momentarily in a side tunnel. When a guard marched past, Indy stepped in front of the surprised Thuggee and delivered a blow to his jaw, dropping him in the dirt. Quickly Indy unhooked the keys from his belt and waved to Willie and Short Round to follow him.

They began to unlock the children's leg irons as fast as possible. At first the children were startled, but when they understood that they had their freedom, their faces came alive with hope. Soon they were breaking each other's chains. In an

explosion of relief and anger, they overwhelmed the guards, then rushed toward the opening in the ceiling. Indy watched as they stormed into the empty temple. In minutes, he knew, they'd find their way to the corridors of the palace and outside to freedom.

For a moment Indy started to follow them, then thought better of it. Palace guards wouldn't be able to stop hundreds of children, but they would be looking for Indy and his friends. So would an angry Mola Ram and the maharajah, wherever they were. Indy peered at the mine cars and the track that led down a dark tunnel.

"Those tracks have to lead out of the mine," he told Willie and Short Round. "All we do is find an empty car and hop a ride."

Short Round kept watch as Indy clambered up a long, narrow conveyor belt for a better view of the mine. The belt moved slowly, carrying large rocks to a crusher above

it. Next to the crusher, a deafening waterfall cascaded into a mammoth cistern, which in turn powered the conveyor belt.

As Indy neared the rock crusher, the conveyor belt suddenly lurched to a stop. Startled, he turned to find a seven-foot Thuggee guard rushing toward him. Before Indy could scramble out of the way, the giant looped an arm around him and pinned him down. Indy squirmed free as the conveyor belt started up again, inching toward the dangerous crusher. He picked up a hammer to clobber the giant. Suddenly Indy felt a searing pain spiralling up his leg. He dropped the hammer helplessly.

Short Round, puzzled and frightened, looked up and saw the maharajah on the ledge above, near the waterfall.

In the maharajah's hand was the krtya doll that looked like Indy. He was stabbing its head with a long, wickedly sharp needle. Indy screamed and clutched his head. The giant Thuggee howled in delight.

Short Round scrambled up to the waterfall. "Give me the doll," he demanded. Smiling, the maharajah looked at him with hollow eyes. He pulled his hand back and then plunged the needle into the krtya's face. As Indy's cries of pain bounced off the tunnel walls, Short Round lunged for the maharajah and wrestled the doll free. He jumped up, grabbed a torch, and thrust it at the maharajah's hand. The young man screamed in pain. Then, very slowly, his face began to change. He looked around groggily. "What happened?"

"Welcome back from the black nightmare of Kali," said Short Round.

When the maharajah realized that Indy and his friends were in danger, he promised to get help. Short Round turned back to the conveyor belt. Indy was his old self as he battled the Thuggee, planting a foot in the giant's stomach and flipping him over. The guard's sash caught in the rock crusher and he was pulled into the machinery, his face twisting in horror.

Willie shouted from below that she'd found an empty mine car. As Short Round hopped in, the car

started down the dusty tracks. Indy hurried after them from a catwalk above, ready to jump in, when suddenly Mola Ram and several guards came thundering after him. He pivoted, unleashing his whip to keep them away, and made the plunge into the streaking mine car. He dropped in next to Willie, safe. Indy was feeling better until gunshots rang out. Two more mine cars, packed with Thuggee guards, were chasing after them. The Thuggees' rifles blazed like cats' eyes in the dark tunnel.

Indy shouted instructions as Short Round seized the brake lever, pushing down on it when they rounded a curve and pulling it up on straightaways. They flew through the darkness.

Short Round ducked as bullets clanged off the metal car. The Thuggees were gaining on them! Indy knew it too. "Slow on the curves!" he yelled to Short Round. "Or we'll fly off the tracks."

Short Round did his best with the brake, but the car was virtually out of control. It was as if they were on a roller coaster, rocketing down the narrow tracks as their stomachs flip-flopped helplessly. At a sharp curve the wheels jumped off the track, then miraculously settled back down. Right behind them the Thuggees loosened their brakes as well. Their rifles kept firing.

"Hold on!" Indy shouted as the ride grew still wilder and the Thuggees kept on gaining. A railroad tie sat under Indy's feet. With Willie's help, Indy heaved it onto the tracks behind them. The faces of the approaching Thuggees showed surprise, then total panic. Their car struck the railroad tie, flew into the air, and careered into the tunnel wall, exploding on impact.

"One down, one to go!" said Indy.

He glanced behind as the other car edged closer. The railroad tracks suddenly forked in two, and the Thuggees pulled onto the second track, parallel to Indy's car. A guard raised a shovel menacingly over his head, aiming at Short Round, but Indy reached over and jerked it away. In the distance Indy spotted a dumper extending down from the mine ceiling, and the lever that would release whatever rocks and debris were inside. As his car hurtled underneath it, Indy struck the dumper lever with his shovel, opening the chute. The Thuggees in the car behind looked up helplessly. They covered their heads, but it was too late. They were buried instantly in a shower of dirt and rocks, and their car slammed to a halt.

"Yippeee!" Short Round shouted with glee.

"Brake, Shorty, brake!" warned Indy.

But when Short Round yanked on the lever, it broke off in his hands. He looked at Indy, frightened. The car hurtled over the tracks ever faster. Thinking quickly, Indy lowered himself over the side of the car. With his foot, he nudged the brake pad under the front wheel back into place. Sparks flew, and the car began to slow.

Suddenly Willie screamed. Indy looked up to find a stone wall looming in front of them. Everyone crouched down, expecting the worst. But the brakes took hold and the car bumped harmlessly into the dead end.

Indy hobbled out of the car, re-

lieved. Down a side tunnel he could see daylight. Safe at last! He looked at his shoe, still smoking from the friction of rubbing against the wheel. "Hey, anybody got some water?" he asked, only half joking.

Before the words died on his lips, a distant rumbling filled the tunnel. Everyone listened warily. The walls began to vibrate, and the ground quaked under their feet. Indy stared down the dark tunnel from which they'd come. His jaw dropped in disbelief. An enormous wall of water thundered toward them ominously like a tidal wave.

"Run! Run!" Indy shouted. It was the cistern, he knew. Somehow Mola Ram and the guards had opened it, hoping to drown them.

The three sprinted toward the light, with the massive wave following at their heels. Short Round's legs began to wobble as he ran in front of Indy. Willie was faltering too, and Indy grabbed her hand. The mouth of the tunnel beckoned wider. With his last ounce of strength, Short Round flung himself through the opening. Indy thrust Willie onto a ledge outside the tunnel and leaped to join her. The water roared out behind them in a giant silver plume, dropping into a deep gorge where crocodiles sunned themselves on flat rocks. The crocodiles looked up angrily at the disturbance.

Indy pointed ahead to the rickety suspension bridge spanning the gorge. "Willie, head for the bridge,"

he said. As they manoeuvered toward it a wild cry came from behind them. Three Thuggee guards wielding swords charged out of the tunnel. Indy quickly pushed Willie and Short Round onto the bridge, then readied his whip.

His first strike coiled around a guard's neck, pulling him down. The second guard, brandishing his sword, shouted wildly as he charged, but Indy's quick fist stopped him. Indy retrieved the sword and held his ground as the last Thuggee attacked. They duelled

desperately until the guard stumbled and fell. Taking the chance to escape, Indy rushed onto the bridge.

Halfway across, he froze. Short Round and Willie were on the other side, held captive by Mola Ram and two muscular guards. A dozen more Thuggees with bows and arrows drawn ringed the hostages. Behind Indy, even more guards thundered out of the mine tunnel.

He was trapped.

"Let my friends go!" Indy shouted to Mola Ram.

The high priest was amused.

"You're in no position to make demands, Dr. Jones."

"You want the stones?" Indy shouted back, holding up his shoulder pouch. "Then let them go free—now."

Mola Ram, growing impatient, spoke in Hindi to the guards, who edged closer to the bridge. "Give me the stones, Dr. Jones."

Indy knew he was badly outnumbered. But even if he surrendered the stones, Mola Ram would probably kill Willie and Short Round. He had to think of something—fast . . .

Without warning, he raised his sword and sliced into the ropes holding the bridge. The rope ends twisted apart, but stopped just short of unravelling completely.

"Very dramatic, Dr. Jones," Mola Ram observed, "but I don't think you'd kill yourself."

"I'd rather do that than give you the stones."

"We shall see." Mola Ram waved his arm. The guards shoved Willie and Short Round onto the bridge with Indy. Their extra weight made the rope ends unravel some more. The bridge sagged and began to sway.

"Now—I want the stones!" shouted Mola Ram.

Indy flashed his sword again, as if daring Mola Ram to act. Enraged, the priest stormed toward the bridge. Indy looked at Short Round and Willie. They were rigid with fear, but Indy got their attention. He wrapped the bottom rope of the bridge around his foot, waiting until they did the same.

Mola Ram, in a trance of rage, didn't notice what Indy had done. As he rushed onto the bridge Indy slashed down with his sword. The ropes unravelled completely, and the bridge fell apart in the middle. Now moored only at the top of the gorge, it was a thread holding four lives together. Thanks to their footholds, Willie and Short Round clung to a dangling rope near the top. Below, Mola Ram and Indy hung side by side, fighting each other. With his free hand, Mola Ram seized Indy's pouch.

Thuggee guards, fearful for their leader as well as the stones, quickly aimed their bows at Indy. The arrows streaked toward their target and landed within inches of Indy's head.

Mola Ram took advantage of Indy's helplessness to pull the stones from the pouch. He smiled in triumph. The stones once more belonged to Kali! But as the high priest clutched them covetously, the stones began to burn his hand. Frightened, he opened his palm and saw that his flesh was seared. He screamed in pain. Then his other hand lost its grip and he fell, shrieking, into the gorge. Indy made a desperate lunge and caught one of the stones. The others, along with the priest, were food for the crocodiles.

The air turned still. Short Round looked up to see that the Thuggees had dropped their weapons and were fleeing. Captain Blumburtt and his troops, with the maharajah be-

side them, were emerging from the mine tunnels to capture the remaining Thuggees. Short Round and Willie waited for Indy as he climbed the fallen bridge to safety.

Standing on the mountain, the three could only look at one another speechlessly, as if they couldn't quite believe what they'd been through—or that they'd all survived.

The next day, borrowing elephants from the maharajah, Indy, Short Round, and Willie journeyed

back to the village in the Mayapore hills. Laughing children rushed to meet them, throwing flowers in their path. The village fields were lush and green again. Indy presented the last Sankara Stone to the old shaman.

"I knew you were coming back," the shaman said, "when life returned to our village."

"That's nice to know," Willie said, "because I had some doubts."

"Come on," Indy said, joking, "you wouldn't have missed this adventure for the world."

Willie smiled. "Maybe you're right. I made two new friends on the way."

"And you prove you one tough lady," said Short Round. He slipped off to watch the elephants play in the river. Tomorrow he and Indy would set out for Delhi, and in a week Short Round would be in his new home, the United States. He couldn't wait. That would be the greatest adventure of them all.